For
Poppy and Coco

Meerkat Choir

NICKI GREENBERG

ALLEN&UNWIN

SYDNEY • MELBOURNE • AUCKLAND • LONDON

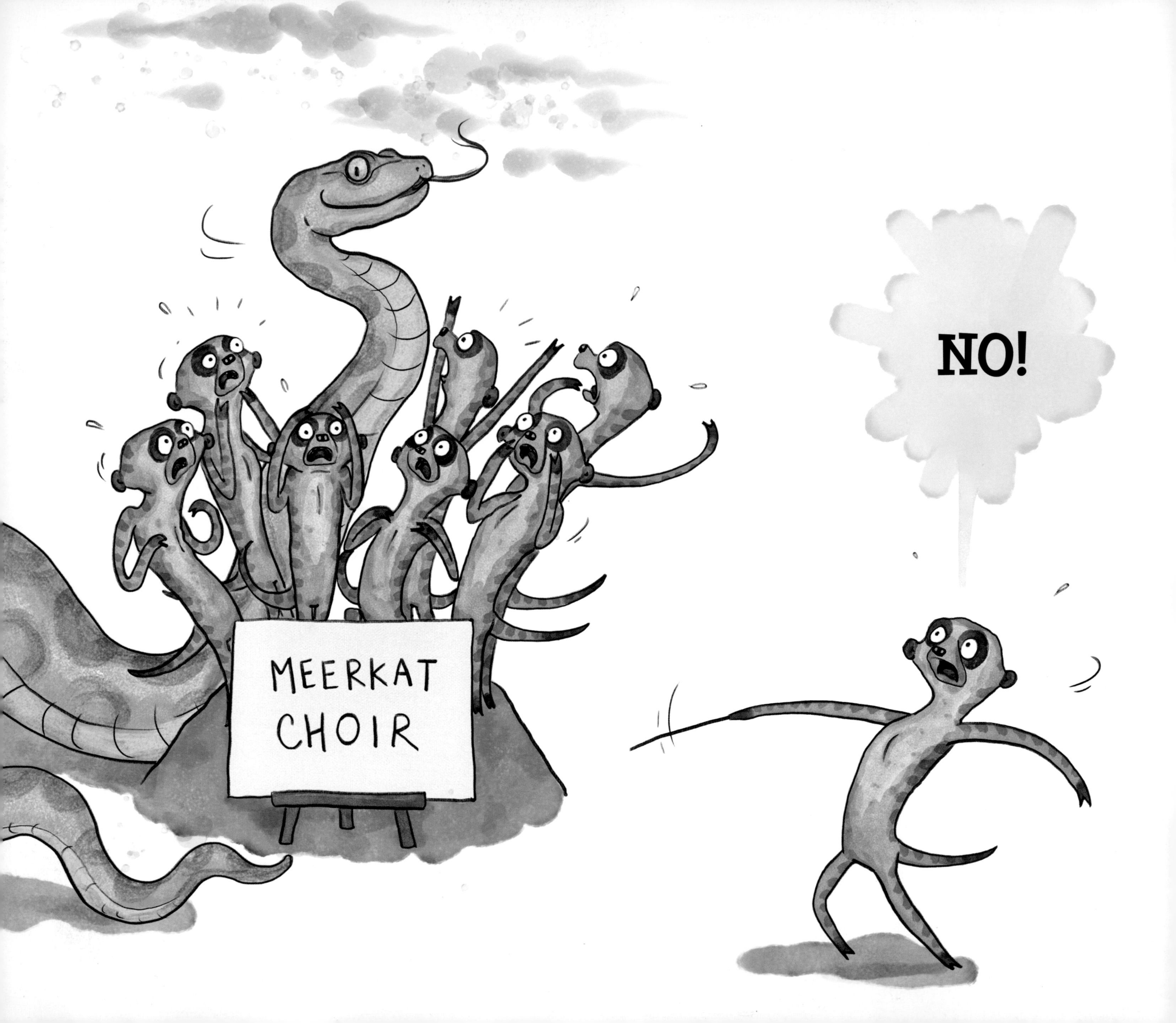
NO!
MEERKAT
CHOIR

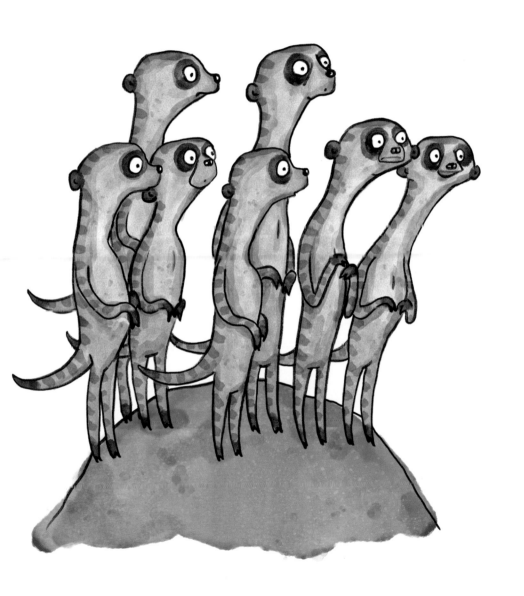

Oh my. Let's try that again, shall we?

MEERKAT CHOIR FULL. GO AWAY!

"Join in!"

First published by Allen & Unwin in 2017

Allen & Unwin
83 Alexander Street
Crows Nest NSW 2065
Australia
Phone: (61 2) 8425 0100
Email: info@allenandunwin.com
Web: www.allenandunwin.com

A Cataloguing-in-Publication entry is available
from the National Library of Australia
www.trove.nla.gov.au

ISBN 978 1 76029 079 5

Cover and text design by Nicki Greenberg and Sandra Nobes
Set in Chowerhead
This book was printed in May 2017 by Everbest Printing Co. Ltd., China.

1 3 5 7 9 10 8 6 4 2

www.nickigreenberg.com